KU-104-959

™

A Book by Hasbro Bradley, Inc.
Pawtucket, Rhode Island 02861
Copyright ©1984 Hasbro Bradley, Inc. and
Walt Disney Productions. All rights
reserved. Printed in the U.S.A. No part
of this book may be reproduced or copied
in any form without written permission
from the copyright owners. Book
designed by Dick Codor and Pegi Goodman.
Written by Mel Gilden and Jymn Magon.
Illustrated by Pat Paris

Butterbear™
Plants a Surprise

Tina was a happy little girl who loved to work in her garden. She liked to dig holes and plant seeds and water the soil. Then she would watch the tender green shoots begin to grow.

One day, she put aside her hoe and went to lie down in a hammock. She wanted to read her new book about a Wuzzle named Butterbear.

Butterbear was a very lovable Wuzzle, half bear and half butterfly.
The bear part of Butterbear loved nature. And the butterfly
part of her loved flowers and plants. So she tended the
beautiful and useful plants that grew in the Land of Wuz.
Often she could be heard talking to her plants.
And though nobody could prove this,
it was said that the plants talked back!

Sometimes, Butterbear invented special
plants for her Wuzzle friends. One time she invented
a special floating sea grass for Moosel so he wouldn't have to
dive to the bottom of the sea to find food. "This time
I've outdone myself," said Butterbear to herself.
"I've invented the perfect plants for
Hoppopotamus and Rhinokey."

Butterbear hummed to herself as she carried Hoppo's gift down the road. The plant was a brand new kind of vegetable tree. Butterbear had invented it because she knew that Hoppopotamus was on a diet. "This plant will solve her salad problems forever! Hoppo will love it!"

When Butterbear got to Hoppo's
House, she rang the doorbell. Hoppopotamus
opened the door and clapped her hands. "Oooh, what's that?"
Butterbear explained, "It's a banana-lettuce tree! A lettuce plant
only grows one head at a time. But I crossed lettuce with
a banana tree so the lettuce would grow in bunches!
You'll have lots of lettuce for your salads now!"
"Great!" shouted Hoppo. "Let's plant
it in my backyard."

In the backyard, Hoppo pulled the paper
and ribbon off the plant. She giggled as
Butterbear planted the tree. "I can hardly
wait until the lettuce bunches grow."
Butterbear wiped her dirty paws.
"That will be soon, Hoppo.
But you must remember
to water it everyday."
Hoppo's smile
faded a bit. "Okay.
But sometimes I'm
forgetful about
watering."

Butterbear went back to her garden for Rhinokey's gift. As she picked up the plant, she chuckled to herself. "Rhinokey likes jokes and tricks. The new plant will be lots of fun for him."

She arrived at Rhinokey's house and rang the doorbell. Instead of a ringing, it made a loud honking sound. "That's Rhinokey for you!" Grinned Butterbear.

Rhinokey answered the door wearing a wastebasket on his head. "How do you like my hat, Butterbear? Ha, ha, ha!"

Butterbear smiled politely. "Very funny, Rhinokey. Speaking of funny, I brought you a silly gift. Can I put it in your backyard?" "Well, I didn't plant on it, but let's grow for it! Ha, ha, ha!"

"What is it?" asked Rhinokey, as he watched Butterbear dig a hole. "It's a watermelon-flower. Bend over and sniff it." When Rhinokey smelled the large flower, it squirted him in the face! "Double great!" laughed Rhinokey. "I'll call it Old Faceful!"

Butterbear was
happy that both her friends
were so pleased with their gifts.
A week later she decided to look in
on the new plants. But when she visited
Hoppopotamus' house, there was trouble.
Hoppo was very upset. "I don't like to complain
Butterbear, but I'm having a problem with my new tree!"

"**W**hat's the matter?" Butterbear said, as they walked to the backyard. "Just look," said Hoppo pointing skyward. Butterbear was shocked! Instead of growing close to the ground, the tree had grown very tall. "The lettuce is so far away, you couldn't reach it with a ladder!" said Butterbear.

"Worse yet," said Hoppo, "the
lettuce bunches are shaped like bananas!"
Butterbear scratched her head. "I don't know what could
have gone wrong, Hoppo. Let me think about this a while, and I'll
come back." When Butterbear left, she headed straight over
to Rhinokey's house. "I hope his plant is doing okay."

But Rhinokey was
upset, too! "I don't like
to look a gift flower in the
petals, Butterbear, but that
new watermelon-flower is a
dud. And that's no joke."
"What seems to be the
matter with the plant?"
asked Butterbear.
"See for yourself," said
Rhinokey. "Go
ahead . . . sniff it."

Butterbear walked over
to the watermelon-flower and
sniffed. It didn't squirt her in
the face. It just dribbled out
a small stream of water.
"It does that all the time,"
said Rhinokey. "That's
about as funny as a
broken joybuzzer."
Rhinokey was upset.
"This bad joke
could ruin my
reputation!"

Poor Butterbear excused herself and walked sadly home. Back in her own garden, Butterbear looked around gloomily. "I'm no good at inventing plants anymore. Why I'm not even fit to tend them! Maybe I should give up gardening entirely!" She broke her garden hoe-backscratcher in two and sat down with a sigh. She was very sad.

Tina leaped from her hammock. "Butterbear can't quit gardening! I think I know an answer. Oh, I wish I was there to help her! I wish, I wish, I wish I was in the Land of Wuz!" Suddenly the sun glittered off a watering can and dazzled Tina so she couldn't see. But when she looked around, she was in Butterbear's garden!

Butterbear sat up with a start. "Who are you?"
"I'm Tina. And I think you're the greatest gardener
in the world." "No, I'm not," frowned Butterbear. "I make crummy
plants." Tina shook her head. "Just because they don't work
the way you wanted doesn't make them crummy.
Maybe if you looked at what the plants really
did, you would see they are great!"

Butterbear suddenly smiled. "I get it!
The plants were meant to do different things!
All I have to do is give the right plant to the right Wuzzle!"
"That's it!" Tina cheered. Butterbear grabbed her shovel
and said, "Come on! We have some switching to
do." Together they ran to Hoppo's house.

Butterbear and Tina ran into Hoppo's backyard and started digging up the banana-lettuce tree. "What are you doing?" cried Hoppo. "Trust me," said Butterbear, lifting one end of the tree.

"And don't worry," Tina said, picking up the other end. "We'll be back!" The two of them scampered off down the street.

When they got to Rhinokey's house,
they found him making faces at himself in
his funhouse mirror. He looked up from his funny
reflection and saw the banana-shaped lettuce. "Say, that's a
yummy-looking plant. Where are you going with it?"
"Your backyard," said Butterbear as Tina
and she ran past him.

Butterbear dug up the watermelon-flower, then plopped Hoppo's tree into the hole. "I'm taking away your dribble flower and giving you this banana-lettuce tree instead. I hope the tree isn't too high for you." Rhinokey smacked his lips. "Lettuce not be silly. Trees are no problem to me. I'm half monkey, you know! Ha, ha, ha!" Rhinokey scampered up the tree with ease and began munching on the new treat.

Butterbear and Tina carried the
watermelon-flower back to Hoppo's house.
Under Hoppo's suspicious eye, the two of them planted it.
Hoppo frowned. "First you give me a lettuce tree that's
too tall. Now you give me a flower that leaks.
Is that supposed to be better?"

"Of course it is," said Butterbear proudly. "With that flower dripping water all the time, you'll never have to remember to water your plants." Hoppo grinned from ear to ear. "That's wonderful! I'll take six more. I want my entire garden watered by watermelon-flowers.!"

Back at her garden, Butterbear gave Tina a
beautiful sunflower-rose. "Thanks for helping
me match the right plants to the right Wuzzles."
Tina smiled. "Well, sometimes you can solve
a hard problem if you just look at it in a new way."
Then Tina gave Butterbear a great big snuzzle.